THE STORM AND THE CALM AFTER IT

KIERA GOPALIA

to all those writers

who helped me fall in love with words

thank you for sharing a piece of yourself with the world

Contents

CHAPTER ONE

THE STORM

and

to anxiety:

every conversation i have becomes your new favorite
song and you play it on repeat,
only pressing pause
once i've analyzed every word.

everyday

you hurt and you lie
and you break me like an ocean wave breaks on the shore

and i keep swimming back because somehow there are
still pieces of me that you have not destroyed.

you are the ocean's current pushing me away
and pulling me right back in

and i am the waves that foolishly curl around you and
refuse to let go.

she

if you were falling, there is no distance
my arms wouldn't reach to catch you.

grew

to the one who stole from me:

i offered you pieces of my soul
without a second thought,
as if i was sure you would give them back. and when you
still needed more,
i dug a little deeper,
pulled out my heart like a weed
and planted it carefully in your hands.

and i've learned that sometimes,
giving everything means nothing

to the person who means everything to you.

back

i'm sorry i built
a home out of you
like you were made of clay. i didn't realize you had
no intention of
inviting me to stay.

the

i burn the crumpled letters that remind me of you,
but i can't seem to forget that you once touched me, too.

leaf

to my weakness:

loving you was a game of tug-of-war. pulling each other in
opposite directions and demanding change
that did not want to come.

so neither of us ever won.
the rope finally tore and
we fell on our backs,
farther apart than where we started.

that

to my dark cloud:

i gazed up at the sky and saw cryptic, mysterious,
powerful. always protecting me.

you were a thunderstorm when the sky was clear and i
chased sidewalks to escape the rain,

shielded my ears
from the sting of thunder, cowered under roofs to avoid
the lightning you threw.

oh, how i wanted to be the sunlight that swallowed your
darkness. how i wanted to be the rainbow after your
storm.

i am strong, but
i cannot stop fury with my bare hands.

was

to the one who is always on my mind:

i miss you most during storms,
when the wind sweeps through my head and scavenges
for the memories of you that
i had carefully placed into cobwebbed corners.

i miss you most during storms,
when the rain seeps into my skin and leaves me yearning
for the words
that once kept me safe and warm.

i miss you most during storms, but if i'm being honest,
i miss you always.

CHAPTER TWO

AND THE CALM AFTER IT

wilting

to the person i was yesterday:

i believe in change,
the change that people don't often notice until it's already
happened
like
petals wilting, eyes reddening,
raindrops evaporating.

i believe in change
that is slow and careful, patiently lingering
like
flowers blooming, pearls forming, hearts healing.

i see little hints of you
tucked in my reflection
and i wonder if you'd be proud of me.

due

to the one who stole from me, (2)

i gave you my happiness by the handful, harvesting pieces
of myself as if i were plucking petals from daisies.
i thought you were my water, my ray of light. but you
were a drought, an eternal night.

i was a field of blooming flowers,
but you tore every stem from their roots and left me with
a barren body.
now i am regrowing my garden and keeping these flowers
for myself.

you washed over me like a wave of darkness and still
expected me to light the sky for you.

to

i was born with an everlasting flame within me
and the fire only grows stronger every time you try to
extinguish my spark.

be careful not to get burned.

the

to the one i fear:

the words on your tongue
only escape when they are angry, spewing rage and spite.
but when they land
on my skin
they turn to joy
because if i let them
collect like dust,
maybe i'll never have the courage to shake them off.
maybe i'll become angry like you, and i don't want to be.
i want to be happy.

i will be happy.

darkness

happiness lives
in a little room in my heart
and some days it
prefers the curtains drawn shut.

and i've learned that's okay.

that

when you left, my heart was broken. i felt pain like a
thousand knives and i cried a thousand tears and
i wrote a thousand poems about you. i'm not telling you
this

to make you feel guilty or
to make you come back.
i'm telling you this because i'm healing,
and i'm doing it on my own.
you left because you thought i was weak,
but your absence made me strong.
like it or not, you've changed me for the better. so i thank
you.

once

to the one who walked away:

i was scared to be without you.
you used to breathe life into my lungs— then suddenly i
had to breathe on my own.

but i've learned i can exist happily without you.

actually, i can flourish without you.

consumed

on days i feel lonely
i remember all the people i let go of because i knew what
was best for me.

and i feel a little less alone
knowing that if no one else has my back, at least i do.

just when i thought i never would, i woke up and felt a
little less pain. i walked a little faster,
stood a little taller,

smiled a little wider.

just when i thought i never could, i put myself back
together.

her

i chase storms without fear because
i know the
dark clouds
will eventually lead to blue skies.